The World According to Dog

The World According to Dog

poems

and teen voices

Joyce Sidman

With photographs by Doug Mindell

Houghton Mifflin Company   Boston

www.houghtonmifflinbooks.com

Book design by Lisa Diercks
The text of this book is set in Mrs Eaves, with Dalliance display.

Library of Congress Cataloging-in-Publication Data
    The world according to dog : poems and teen voices / by Joyce Sidman.
        p. cm.
    Summary: A collection of poems about dogs is accompanied by essays by young people about the dogs in their lives.
    ISBN 0-618-17497-4
    1. Dogs—Literary collections. [1. Dogs—Literary collections. 2. Youth's writings.]
I. Sidman, Joyce.
    PZ5 .W78 2003
    810.8'03629772—dc21
    2002000476

Printed in Singapore
TWP 10 9 8 7 6 5 4 3 2

To Merlin, of the black silk ears,
And Pecos, who came before

        —J. S.

To my parents, June and Gene,
who always encouraged me to be creative
and who thoughtfully included the "u" in my name

        — D. M.

Contents

Awakening

I dream of deep-sea
fishing: awake to find dog
breathing in my face.

Always Take a Dog

~~

Go out walking.
In some part of every day,
step into the waiting arms
of the sky and whisk away—
but always take a dog,
so that you have something to follow.

Stroll or saunter,
steam up hills, thoughts rumbling
through your head like bees
bent on their own courses—
but always take a dog,
so you can watch how he chooses
which path to take.

Absorb the light:
the sun-splayed distance,
the close, soft dampness
of a cloudy day—
but always take a dog,
so you can see how
the wind moves through his fur.

Be alert for what the day
might offer you: a gull, a penny,
the pale thumbprint of moon—
but always take a dog,
so you can heed how
his nose moves from side to side,
seeking unexpected treasure.

The Usual Spots

Spring
Trembling at the door
  wanting Out
Mud-faced and weary
  wanting In

Summer
Panting fat tongue in
Smooth   cool   garage

Autumn
Nowhere
  Everywhere
    Stalking
      Scattering
        Bearing bits of leaves

Winter
Regal atop
  a snowdrift
Curled like a cat
    inside a window-square
    of sun

Hey, Comet!

∽∽

Anna Engstrom, age 12

My four-legged friend is Comet. At school we would call him a "genius of his genus," but at home we say, "Hey, Comet!"

After receiving Comet, we realized that our dog had a lot to learn:

1. *Our house is not a bathroom*
2. *Fetch*
3. *Puppy eyes = good stuff*
4. *Jumping off the dock*

Comet's greatest accomplishment is probably fetch. Our dog has speed, and caught on to catching the ball very fast.

At our cottage, we would throw his toy into the water from the shore and he would retrieve it. Soon we began throwing his toy off the dock, but Comet still ran back to the shore to enter the water from there. Now Comet knows he won't snap in two if he jumps off the dock.

Comet is timid, especially around other canines. However, when he is playing fetch with his ball, YOU'RE ON HIS

Comet

black lab/blue heeler mix,
age 3

TURF! He does not bite or growl — he just stares at you with those puppy eyes and intelligent smile, as if to say, "Come near my toy and you'll regret it."

Comet is the best dog. I wouldn't trade him for the world, because he is *my world.*

How to Meet a New Idea (Based on the Study of a Dog)

—*after May Swenson*

Detect from a distance.

Test the air.
Approach with interest:
ears open,
eyes bright.

Remain neutral.
Circle carefully so as to view from all sides.

Do not speak.
Keep head low, respectful.
Refrain from growling.

Sniff thoroughly.

If acceptable, wag tail.
If not, lift leg.

Noses

Mine
is an afterthought,
a molehill,
a period between
two sentences of eyes.

Yours
is the main event:
a long, elegant,
labyrinthine
echo chamber of smell.

I
might detect
wet earth,
rank fists of marigolds,
the distant tsunami
of skunk.

You
are sorting out
the relative age of
squirrels
that passed this way
last week.

I live
for bright quilts
of color,
the inflection of voices,
ciphers on a page.

You're sifting
the mystery
of invisible breezes,
messages
from hoof and beak.

Wouldn't it be fine
if,
for a moment,
we could switch places?
You could see
the distant stars.

And I could dive
through
that ocean of smell,
finding answers to
questions
I've never asked.

Bandy

∽∽

Sarah Milnar, age 13

This is the story of a dog named Bandy. She was what some people like to call a mutt. You know, the kind of dog that has a shaggy coat and a short stubby tail, and so many different colors of brown, gold, and gray that you get dizzy if you look at them too long. The kind of dog that always seemed out of place, no matter where you went.

*When my mother was a girl, she was a bit like Bandy; not the most popular pup in the litter, didn't get the best grades, did not have the latest fashions, which every girl at her school just **had** to have. She also walked to school, which was considered very uncool.*

She made her way home one afternoon, having had the worst possible day. Bad grade on a math test, lost her history essay, had forgotten her lunch — need I say more? It was just a rotten day. She rounded the corner and saw a very peculiar sight: a large box labeled FREE PUPPIES. Inside the box was one little mutt that no one seemed to have wanted.

She couldn't stand to leave it there, so she took the little puppy out of its box. Immediately it began to lick her face. It was love at first sight. At that instant my mother knew she was going to keep it. My mother decided to call her Bandy, because she found her abandoned.

Although there are no remaining photos of Bandy, her memory will live on forever. She helped my mother understand the importance of life and affection. She guided my mother to appreciating everything and everyone as much as possible.

Our thanks to the person who left her there.

At the Last Minute

At the last minute
something addles the brain.
Plans are made, bags are packed,
the car is in the driveway,
when the descent into
utter madness
begins.
Due at the airport in an hour,
I frantically try to tame
Neanderthal hair and
cover three new zits
on a nose the size
of China's Great Wall.
I rant and rave, cursing gods
who hide essential clothing,
then pray (unanswered) for a new body—
or at least one that will allow me
to button my favorite jeans.
When I have finally
found
      my
          wits,
I go looking for
the One Who Must Stay Behind.
I find him dealing with the moment
in his own way:
panting,
grinning,
digging up
a mess of
dead
skunk.

Tag

Dog and toad play tag
under the spring junipers.
I fear for the toad.

The Banner
of Dog

∞

Behold the banner of Dog
flapping in the breeze:
four pawprints and a burr
on a mud-brown field.

He who defends it
shows no stiff ruff
nor growling gait.
Instead, tail reeling

like a windmill,
he bows to his attacker,
rolls over
shamelessly,

and offers up his
secret weapon:
charm. In the end,
all swear allegiance.

Behold the banner of Dog
waving in the sun:
four pawprints and a burr
on a mud-brown field.

Rusty
the Squirrel
Exterminator

∽

Karen Ann Stahlheber,
age 15

Standing on the porch with a small, nondescript terrier at my feet, I scan the yard purposefully. My eyes spot a squirrel innocently crouching in the middle of the yard. Without moving, I whisper softly, "Go get it." A red-grizzled streak shoots across the lawn, barking up a storm. The dog chases the squirrel up a tree and continues barking. I call out his name for ten full minutes before deciding it is useless. I walk out to the lawn, catch the still-barking dog under my arm, and take him into the house.

Motivated solely by food, love, and small vermin, my dog Rusty is a constant source of amusement. Within a few months of his arrival, he had eaten an entire lemon pie and a whole bag of chocolates. Needless to say, I have learned a lot since he arrived. I have learned to put all food away, to push the chairs in at the table, and, most importantly, never to leave a meal unattended for any length of time. I have also learned the location of every other dog in the neighborhood. I have discovered exactly what a dog's idea of "helping" with homework is, and how comforting a squirrel-chasing, book-hogging, face-licking, pie-scarfing little terrier's presence can be.

Rusty

border terrier, age 2

Dog and Squirrel: Steps in a Flirtation

The bushy flick of your tail
catches my attention.
> *I am aware of your presence,*
> *but I am ignoring you.*

You are now my bull's-eye.
This will be a fine game.
> *It may be a game,*
> *but I set the rules.*

Whenever you lower your guard,
I step forward.
> *I never lower my guard.*
> *All escape routes are intact.*

My body is an arrow
pointing at your heart.
> *O large clumsy one,*
> *have you any idea how fast I can run?*

I draw closer.
The space between us is nothing.
> *Odd how the sunlight*
> *kindles your dark fur.*

I can taste the silk of your tail.
You can't possibly get away now.
> *I know the precise point at which*
> *I must flee. Still, those eyes . . .*

Gaze locked, I pounce!
And you are . . .
> *Gone, of course.*
> *My heart pounds! See you tomorrow?*

Stink

I am trying to understand this.
I am standing with the hose in one hand
and the other grabbing
the scruff of your neck,
trying to understand this.
The shampoo streaks
across your back like honey,
and the foam coats my furious legs,
and the cold, cold water
pumped from two hundred feet down
chills us both;
and I am trying to understand this
ecstasy of stink that has me
retching but made you
dive and roll, eyes closed in bliss,
feet waving at the sun,
oblivious to my voice,
as if you had discovered
all the world's wealth in a single spot
and wanted nothing more
than to share
its bright gold.

Of a Dog

∾

Scott Austen Robinson,
age 14

Growing up in a family of dog lovers, I had no choice but to carry this title as I grew up. Please, don't get me wrong: I love dogs. Our family has two on our ranch; one is a German shepherd mix and the other is of unknown breed, but he looks remarkably like a coyote. Blackjack (the shepherd mix) is my mom's and, of course, spoiled rotten. Ace, however (if you haven't already guessed, he's our other dog), would rather run off chasing a deer and come home smelling completely foul than be pampered. If you have a dog, you probably know what I mean by "foul." A dog has some strange instinct to find the worst-smelling carcass within a two-mile radius, roll in it, trot home, and expect to be loved all the more for doing so. More often than not, I'm afraid, Ace is greeted by gagging and is immediately escorted back outside.

What I have found to be the strangest thing about Ace is his choice of toys. Most people think of a tennis ball or a rubber squeaky vegetable as a dog toy. Not me. Oh, for Blackjack, sure, but Ace? Nah, he would much rather play tug-o'-war with a ripped-up shirt. You may think

Ace

collie/husky mix, age 5

this sounds strange, but believe me, I know. I have spent many hours of my life running through pastures with Ace. I'll usually be desperately holding on to my end of what once was my favorite shirt or pair of shorts. When I finally collapse with exhaustion (it's always me; try as I might, I can never tire my companion), he is barely panting, and in his mouth is a now-unidentifiable rag.

Hornet's Nest

Troublemaker
shoving your nose
where it shouldn't be
they got you all right
must have been thirty
burrowing all over your fur
shoving in
those ugly teardrop stingers
I had to scrape them
from your skin with a stick
your eyes so wild
so blank so full of pain
over and over
kept finding more
even when we got indoors
and your nose
began swelling
like a laundry bag
I pulled a dead one
from your burning ear

Understand
I tried to draw their fire
but they'd marked you out
all they wanted was
you, you, you

Separation

Vacation: two weeks
away from you.
Every town had a dog,
and every one of them
came to smell your scent
on my clothes.
One chased planes.
One limped apologetically.
One had fur the color
of hot cocoa.
None of them
reminded me of you.

There was a seal in a zoo,
though, rescued from death,
who lay plump and sleek
on the stones of his enclosure.
His liquid eyes
followed his trainer
as yours follow me,
suspecting something
taking place
in a world
beyond his reach.

Understanding

Of all my friends, dog

is often the only one

who understands me.

Dog in Bed

Nose tucked under tail,
you are a warm, furred planet
centered in my bed.
All night I orbit, tangle-limbed,
in the slim space
allotted to me.

If I accidentally
bump you from sleep,
you shift, groan,
drape your chin on my hip.

O, that languid, movie-star drape!
I can never resist it.
Digging my fingers into your fur,
kneading,
        I wonder:
How do you dream?
What do you adore?
Why should your black silk ears
feel like happiness?

This is how it is with love.
Once invited,
it steps in gently,
circles twice,
and takes up as much space
as you will give it.

Morning Greeting

Casey O'Malley, age 12

Our old stairs creak whenever you walk on them, sagging under the weight of age. Their noise is the only sound in the morning. Everything seems asleep. But when I peer down to the floor, I see a flutter of cheerful wakefulness. A ginger-colored dog comes wriggling up, happy just to see me. Her fur takes on a brilliant shine in the morning, and her endearing brown eyes penetrate right into me. I smile as she paws my feet and waits for me to pet her.

But she isn't satisfied with a simple, superficial pat. With her nose she'll push me over to a chair and wait for me to sit down, her tail wagging furiously all the while. She sets her smiling face on my knee and looks up into my eyes as I massage her velvety ears and murmur, "Good dog . . . what a good puppy." Then we'll both just sit there in wordless understanding. After a few silent minutes, she'll lumber back to her dog bed, plop down, and set her head on its rim, watching me with a look of serene devotion.

Freya

golden retriever, age 3

What Your Ears Remind Me Of

∽

Camouflaged entrances to
a secret underground cavern.

The beard of a Sikh warrior,
the tail of his steed.

The lazy fold of the sleeve
of some royal garment.

Grandma's antique bone-china
gilt-edged Wedgwood teacups.

A windy beach, scored with
ripples of sand and sea.

A conch shell, curled and pink,
waiting for whispers.

A lap I used to press
against while weeping.

Ninja

〜

Arielle Dekofsky, age 14

I remember the day my mom called us to come see a poodle puppy who had been abandoned. He was near death and had no will to live; he had stopped eating or taking water. We held and comforted him, all the while coaxing him to lick water and food from our fingers. Slowly he began to lift his head and show signs of a willingness to fight for life.

On the way home, he slept soundly in my arms. He was weak, like a skeleton, and I felt a tremendous responsibility for him. We named our rescue puppy Ninja because he always slipped away in the shadows, hidden by his black coat, watching us longingly but not understanding exactly what we were all doing. But as time went on, Ninja would cautiously approach us, slowly inching his way, making his space in our family.

Ninja has chosen to make his mark by stealing. Nothing is safe, nothing is sacred. He is particularly fond of my hair accessories. He devours all that he can find and promptly regurgitates everything for me to discover. Many mornings I must choose my hairstyle according to what he has not consumed. He desires mainly my possessions: one such thing

Ninja

standard poodle, age 4

was a frog finger puppet. This frog made its way all through Ninja's system, which I believe is a medical phenomenon. My mom was on "pooper-scooper duty" and noticed that one of the scoops had big bulging eyes and green feet sticking out.

I wake up every morning and know if we had not saved him that day, he surely would have died. Now, Ninja claims our brick bench outside as his throne, sitting like a gargoyle atop an ancient castle wall, ever vigilant, protecting the family he loves, and his princess — me.

Puppy Love

He is everything,
this boy I met today:
blinding sunlight,
dark mysterious caves,
over-the-top scent of lilac,
grace of swan,
languid puissance of jaguar.
He stills my breath,
sets my heart vaulting madly.

We haven't spoken yet.

By the way,
he has your eyes.

Foot Fetish

My feet sometimes
start dancing by themselves:
white-socked toes
bobbing on the couch
like marshmallows.
You stalk them quietly;
brown eyes tracking,
muzzle dipping
back and forth
to the music in my head.

Who can explain what happens
when you finally pounce?
The fierce bites that never land?
The socks damp
with the tickle of teeth?
The joy of growling
at someone
you love?

The One
Who Listens

∽

Paige Herfurth Marvin,
age 13

The relationship between dogs and teenagers is like no other. After a hard and miserable day at school, a dog is waiting for you to come home. No matter what kind of mood you are in, your dog is there for you. A dog is like a journal. You can confess your deepest, darkest secrets and be confident that your dog won't tell a single soul. A dog will slither under your bed sheets when you're scared of the dark. A dog will sleep at the edge of your bed to watch for monsters. A dog cares and loves you as much as you love her.

Tilly

boxer, age 8

This Is a Secret

and has the
potential for extreme
embarrassment,
but the truth is
that,
after I've navigated
a day of
pointless assignments,
fake smiles,
and crowded, shoving hallways,
I long only to
discard my life — everything in it —
and bury myself
in the deep armchair
of your smell.

The Splash of Your Heart

Watching you
greet strangers
is like watching a diver
spring off the board
humbly and with grace
trusting the blue air
and the depths
of love

I want to
gather you back
midair
that handful of puppy
you once were
keep you curled
in my palm
never hear the splash
of your heart
hitting
the world

Sadie

∾

Michelle Aaberg, age 12

Sadie has a free spirit and a lively soul. She broke both of her back leg tendons by playing with balls over and over again, and chasing horses. She just can't stop. Sadie had a big green ball and she would play with it till she died if you let her. Chasing horses is just in her blood. She still follows us around when we do horse chores.

Sadie has also developed a tumor on the back of her right shoulder. It does not seem to affect her strong and powerful will. The vet said we should have lost her two years ago during Christmas, but she is still on her four legs and kicking. There is not much that can help her, so we just let her live her life and not poke and prod at her with those technical vet things.

It's her strong spirit that keeps her alive today. She just won't give up. Even if she died, her spirit would still be with me.

Sadie

red Australian shepherd,
age 8

Happiness

Winter sky today:

close, soft, furled: a blue-eyed dog

curled on a pillow.

Dog Lore

Whatever shrieks the loudest
is the most satisfying to pursue.

A growl's cadence says more
than the growl itself.

To gather a whole day's sun,
one must be prepared to shift places.

Patience and intensity
open the most doors.

Speed makes the ears fly;
licks make the tongue happy.

Touch is the only true comfort.

Madeline

∽

Alexandra Seydow, age 15

My dog, Madeline, is wise for her age, considering she's only ten. She's learned a life lesson that many of us have yet to learn: how to accept who she is.

If you were to see Madeline from a distance, she would appear to be no more than a large cotton-ball puff with a thick waist and four short stumps growing from her belly. She doesn't care that she wasn't blessed with the body of a supermodel. She simply wags her tail and announces proudly: "Love me, love my flaws; I am the best thing since doggy doors."

Her fur reminds me of the Arctic; she looks much like a tiny walrus wearing an Eskimo coat. A rather strange sight, but oddly it draws you in for a closer look. Most days her hair behaves in this wild way, yet Madeline doesn't shy away in her cage. She's never heard of a bad hair day.

If my dog could offer one piece of advice she would say, "There are no standards, no perfect person. There is only us, the way God molded us. Why mess with God's wishes? He is wiser than we will ever be."

Madeline

bichon frisé, age 10

Bully Lessons

I remember each one:
the sausage-sized Dachshund
that bit your nose;
the Great Dane that
fired his volley of pee;
the barrel-chested Vizsla
that tackled you like a linebacker,
then held you down,
his ears back, fangs exposed,
paw against your belly—
rumbling that
eternal
lesson.

Do you keep these
incidents in mind?
Do you hold
fear close, hunching
your body to hide it?
Do you lower
your gaze before the world,
guarding against
all possible insults?

Or do you trot out
to meet the day,
refusing to learn from
such bully lessons:
eyes gleaming like chestnuts,
ears cocked to the breeze,
moist nose aloft,
bearing its tiny
sickle of scar?

How I Felt When My First Dog Died

∽∾

Christopher Christenson,
age 15

When I was about ten, my family wanted to get me a dog for my birthday. We lived in a not-so-great neighborhood, so we needed a watchdog. We got the dog from the pound the day before he was going to be put to sleep (talk about a lucky dog). He was a little black Scottish terrier, and he looked like the dog Dorothy had in The Wizard of Oz. *My mom named him Toto. Since he was my dog, I was responsible for training him. I taught him to sit, stay, speak, fetch, and nip at people if they came into our yard. We became really close friends.*

About a year later, on his birthday and the day before mine, something tragic happened. Being like any other dog, he saw a squirrel and went tearing off after it. He tore right through the gate that was accidentally left open, with me running after him. He followed the squirrel right into the middle of traffic, with me stopping at the curb and staring in horror as he chased the thing right down the road. The next thing I knew, he was rolling down the street. A car had hit him. The man who hit him stopped for a moment and then drove off, leaving my dog in the street. I went over to see if Toto was okay, but as I picked him up and walked back to the sidewalk, he licked my face and died right in my arms.

Now I have a new dog, but she will never be the same as my Toto. I love the new dog, and they both mean a lot to me, but I still think about Toto.

Shedding

I sleep, warm, under
its soft scattering;

breathe it, wear it
on shirt and trousers.

Sometimes I wonder
how much of it I eat;

how much becomes
this tissue, these bones.

It is everywhere, placed
mysteriously as God,

woven into life without
knowledge or understanding.

Sweeping it from my pillow,
I have even cursed it;

but I think it will endure.
The other night I held

a long, pale strand to the light—
not black, like yours—

a memory of the dog
who came before.

Honey, Cream, and Licorice

So much doesn't seem fair
in this world.
So much seems off kilter.
Love, trust, happiness

seem flung upon us
in a fool's measure:
heaps in one corner,
elsewhere, barren earth.

To right wrongs
is to enter a swampland
of scant hummocks
and sucking pools.

In the neighborhood park,
far away from it all
yet somehow smack
in the heart of things,

a trio of dogs lick noses.
One, the color of cream,
another of honey,
the third a deep black licorice.

Three dogs
in the spring sun,
licking noses. Briefly
this tottering world
                    rights itself.

What Really Matters

༄

Maria Louise Petrella,
age 18

Our family dog, Lucky, slows me down when life gets complicated and reminds me that events are only as complex as I make them. He will place his head on my lap, and as I gently stroke him, he will release a deep sigh, taking all my stress away. He makes me enjoy the simple moments in life, like walking outside on a warm spring day or running across a rolling meadow. His pleasure in doing things for fun puts my life into perspective. I don't want to spend my life doing something I hate in order to obtain material possessions. Lucky is a constant reminder that I don't have to.

Lucky

lab/shepherd/Samoyed mix,
age 2

Doggy Bag

dog days: the hottest time of the year ☙ **dogdom:** the world of dogs or dog fanciers; dogs collectively ☙ **dog-eared:** the corner of a page turned down or creased by careless use ☙ **dog-eat-dog:** viciously competitive ☙ **dogfight:** a fight in close quarters, especially between two airplanes ☙ **dogged:** difficult to deal with; stubborn, obstinate ☙ **doggerel:** undignified rhyming poetry ☙ **doggone:** darned, confounded ☙ **doggy bag:** a package of leftovers ☙ **dogleg:** a golf fairway that bends to the right or left ☙ **dogless:** having no dog ☙ **dog paddle:** a beginner's swimming stroke ☙ **dog's age:** a very long time ☙ **dogsbody:** a person given a variety of menial tasks ☙ **dog's life:** a life of constant work and drudgery ☙ **Dog Star:** Sirius, the brightest of the fixed stars ☙ **dog-tired:** utterly exhausted ☙ **dogwatch:** a night shift ☙ **go to the dogs:** be ruined ☙ **in the doghouse:** in disfavor ☙ **let sleeping dogs lie:** refrain from stirring up trouble ☙ **seadog:** an old, seasoned sailor ☙ **sundogs:** bright lights that appear on either side of the sun on cold days ☙ **teach an old dog new tricks:** try to teach someone who is set in his or her ways ☙ **watchdog:** someone who protects or guards safety and integrity ☙ **work like a dog:** to work hard, unceasingly

Merlin

poetry muse, Gordon setter,
age 7

Note to the Reader

This book started with a dog — my dog. I began writing poems about him in a dark time, when I needed comfort and he was there. Friends, reading the poems, told me their feelings about their dogs, which spurred me to create more poems. When my editor read the collection, she asked a "What if?" question: "What if we were to ask teens to write about their dogs, and include those stories with the poems?"

I posted invitations on listserves and teen Web sites. Librarians and teachers across the country helped me. The essays that flooded in were so full of warmth that I knew teen voices belonged in the book. The teen authors provided photos of their dogs, and then Doug Mindell — with his emotive, expressive photographs — illustrated my poems.

That is how this book came together. But it started with a dog.

— J. Sidman